little Miss Giggles

by Roger Hargreaves

Published by Thurman Publishing Limited
The Mill Trading Estate Acton Lane London NW10

Can you giggle and eat cornflakes at the same time?

Little Miss Giggles could!

Do you giggle while you're asleep?

Little Miss Giggles did!

Can you giggle while you're brushing your teeth?

Little Miss Giggles could!

She was the giggliest girl in the world, and she lived in Chuckle Cottage.

But, one terrible day last summer, you'll never guess what happened.

She lost her giggle!

Just like that!

Gone!

She had woken up giggling.

As usual.

She had giggled her way downstairs.

As usual.

And she had giggled while she was having breakfast.

As usual!

But, while she was out walking in the woods around Chuckle Cottage, she realised that she wasn't giggling.

She stopped.

"That's odd," she thought to herself.

Now, ordinarily, she would have giggled to herself.

But not today.

She tried.

Nothing happened!

She tried again.

Nothing happened again!

"Oh dear," she thought, miserably.

And, as she walked along, a little tear trickled down her cheek.

She met Mr Happy who was out for his usual morning stroll.

"Hello little Miss Giggles," he laughed. "And how are we today?"

But then he noticed her sad little face.

"What's happened?" he asked, anxiously. "You're the happiest person I know!"

He paused.

"Next to myself of course," he added hastily.

"I've lost my giggle," she explained, miserably.

"Lost your giggle?" he asked in bewilderment.

Mr Happy scratched his head.

"Mmm," he said. "Well, we'll just have to find it again, won't we?"

Little Miss Giggles nodded, but not very hopefully.

"Come on," he said and, seizing her by the hand, he took her off to see Mr Funny.

"There's nobody like Mr Funny for a giggle," he said.

But it was no use.

Mr Funny tried and tried to produce a giggle, even a chuckle, or even a smile, but little Miss Giggles just couldn't.

"Tell you what," said Mr Funny. "I'll tell you my very latest joke!"

"Made it up myself," he added modestly. "Very funny!"

He could hardly get to the end of the joke for laughing, and, when he had finished, both he and Mr Happy nearly fell over they were laughing so much.

But not little Miss Giggles!

"It's no use," she sighed. "I'm going to be miserable for the rest of my life, I know I am!"

Then she thought.

"And I'll have to change my name," she sobbed.

And she started to cry again.

Big fat tears!

Oh dear me!

So, Mr Happy took her to see Mr Topsy Turvy to ask his advice.

"Morning good," he said cheerfully, and then he caught sight of little Miss Giggles's sad face.

"Matter the what's?" he asked.

He always spoke back to front!

Mr Happy explained what had happened.

"Dear oh!" he exclaimed.

Then he thought.

"Doctor," he said. "Doctor the see to her take!"

"That's a good idea," said Mr Happy, and took her straight away to see Doctor Makeyouwell.

Mr Happy told the doctor all about little Miss Giggles's lack of giggle.

"Mmm," he said. "Put out your tongue!"

"Not you, you Silly Billy!" he said to Mr Happy.

Little Miss Giggles put out her tongue.

"Looks all right to me," said Doctor Makeyouwell. "Open your mouth!"

Doctor Makeyouwell peered inside.

"Mmm," he said again. "You're right! Not a giggle in sight!"

"I'm sorry," he added, "but there's nothing I can do for you. You'll just have to wait for your giggle to come back!"

Poor little Miss Giggles!

Mr Happy took her home, and even he by this time was not looking his cheerful self.

What a sorry sight!

Don't you think?

"Why don't you try to giggle?" he said hopefully.

Little Miss Giggles opened her mouth.

"Ha ha ha," she said, dolefully.

"Hee hee hee," she said, miserably.

"Ho ho ho," she added, mournfully.

It was no use.

No use at all!

"I'm sorry I can't help," said Mr Happy as they reached the garden gate of Chuckle Cottage.

And, as little Miss Giggles went sadly through her front door, he went home.

To think.

The IDEA came to him while he was having lunch.

He rubbed his hands with glee.

"Tee hee," he chortled to himself.

And, later that afternoon, he knocked on the front door of Chuckle Cottage.

"Who's there?" asked a sad little voice.

"It's me," called out Mr Happy. "I have a present for you!"

Little Miss Giggles, looking thoroughly miserable, opened the door.

"Here you are," said Mr Happy, and handed her a large box.

On top of the box, in large letters, it said:

'1 GIGGLE
MEDIUM SIZE
THIS SIDE UP
HANDLE WITH CARE'

Little Miss Giggles looked at the box in amazement.

"What is it?" she asked.

"What it says it is," laughed Mr Happy.

"You lost your giggle, so I have got you another one!"

"That giggle cost me a lot of money," he added.

Little Miss Giggles opened the box.

"But there's nothing in it," she exclaimed.

"Of course not," said Mr Happy. "Giggles are invisible!"

"But that's absolutely ridiculous," said little Miss Giggles.

"Is it?" chuckled Mr Happy.

"Of course it is!" she giggled.

She giggled!

She GIGGLED!!